Halloween Fun

For JAMB
—M. M.

ISBN-13: 978-0-545-10432-6
ISBN-10: 0-545-10432-7

12 11 10 9 8 7   13/0

Printed in the U.S.A.   40

First Scholastic printing, October 2008

Designed by Sammy Yuen Jr.

The text of this book is set in Century Schoolbook.

Halloween Fun

Written by Margaret McNamara
Illustrated by Mike Gordon

Ready-to-Read
SCHOLASTIC INC.
New York Toronto London Auckland Sydney
Mexico City New Delhi Hong Kong Buenos Aires

Jamie was having a
Halloween party.
All the first graders came.

Katie was a ghost.

Neil, Reza, and Becky
were pirates.

Emma was an elevator.

"This is a great party!"
said Ayanna.

"Wait till you see
the fun house!" said Jamie.

"Wow!" said Reza.

"Yo ho!" said the pirates.

"Up, please," said Emma.
They went through the door.

"It is your turn, Hannah,"
said Jamie.

The fun house
did not look
so fun to Hannah.

It was
dark.

It was creepy.

"I want to go," said Hannah.
"And I also do not."

"Hmm," said Jamie.
"What if we went together?"

Jamie held Hannah's hand.
They went into
the fun house.

Hannah felt a spider web.
"Eek!" she cried.

"The web is fake,"
said Jamie.

"And the spiders
are plastic."

They put their hands
in a bowl of goopy worms.
"Yuck!" said Hannah.

"Those are candy worms
in Jell-O," said Jamie.

"Yum, raspberry,"
said Hannah.

Finally, they saw a WITCH!

"That is my mom!"
said Jamie.
"Hello, Hannah,"
said Jamie's mom.

"Happy Halloween."
She gave Hannah
a bag of candy.

The fun house was done.
"How was it, Hannah?"
asked Jamie.

"Can we go again?"
asked Hannah.

"I did not know
how much fun
I was missing!"